Ms Lily
& the Pterodactyl

Author
Malcolm S Urquhart

Illustrator
Yvette Gilbert

Thanks to everyone for the encouragement and support on my first story, you're all magic.

It was a shop like no other. Why? Because you couldn't buy anything in it. It had the musty smell like my grandad's cupboard under the stairs. The shop was dark and forbidding ... nobody ever ventured into it as the things inside may not want you to open that little door with the wobbly black handle. The things just sulked undisturbed in their misery.

Regardless of the weather that day or on any other day for that matter, little gusts of wind outside the shop developed into dust devils.Then, just like that, they vanished ! Out of sight! Gone, only to reappear, some said, at the edge of Ginkgo Forest.

The outside of the shop was black, not only was it black but it also seemed to sneer at all passers-by who would veer away from the shop front as they passed fearing something would reach out, catch them by their legs and drag them into the darkness...

It did exactly this to Miss.Lily, 100 years ago. The story was on the lips of everyone in the little town but not just because of her disappearance..

The Creaking Parlour and Ms. Lily are forever entwined. She was nicknamed, 'The Bird Lady of Crescent Moon'' on account of the mysterious goings on in her old riverbank cottage.

Miss Lily nurtured many different birds in her humongous nest of hair.

You could count up to ten birds at any one time. That was a lot of hair! Right? They were mostly crows, blackbirds, baby sea eagles, barn owls, tawny owls, long eared owls. The owls were amazing and could keep‐ a 360 degree lookout for unwanted predators. Sometimes you could find geese, lapwings, oystercatchers, even woodpeckers, mallards, blue tits, blackbirds, a tiny wren in that crowded nest on top of her head, and once upon a time, it was home to a baby pterodactyl.

A what???? Yup, you heard it right. A baby flying dinosaur!

Pterodactyl means a winged finger! Imagine if you had wings on your fingers!

She called him Herbert. It was her late husband's name. Herbert the pterodactyl made an almighty screech whenever he came round the riverbend, at top speed mind, and spotted Miss Lily.

Caaaawwaaaaaaaaaaaaaawwwwwwwwwkkkkkkk!!!!!!!!,
he would sing.

This noise (So loud you'd have to cover your ears) could be heard as far as the Tithonian mountain's...a long way away! In fact, the screech was so loud that toads would bounce out of the water high enough to be caught by Herbert's beak. Yum yum! Delicious 😋!!

Herbert sang,
Cawwaaaaawwwwwwwwwwwwwwwwwwwkkkkkk!!!!!!!
over and over! He was always so excited to see Ms Lily at the end of a long day's fishing.

Sometimes orphaned chick's seemed to appear out of nowhere. Kind Miss Lily took great care over them so they could find a cosy place on top of her head in the nest of her beautifully grown hair. It was so safe and warm they could curl up and drift off to sleep in seconds . Especially Herbert, he was the quickest of all the birds/dinosaurs/reptiles to fall asleep at night. Mind you, he could eat over 100 fish per day, so he'd probably be very tired.

Miss Lily was a very caring soul. Tragedy had visited her

in her early–years. She now preferred the company and souls of her birds. She could mimic the calls of over 50 birds, just by changing the shape of her mouth. Whenever she called them the birds returned to her on the riverbank.

As for Herbert, well, he was a bit of a different story when it came to getting him in for the night. Sure, he spent most of his days hoovering up bouncing toads, sometimes he'd plunge into the river to gulp down schools of fresh trout. Delicious!

Every day when the sun was setting, when the riverbank was bedding down for the night and the voles were getting comfy in their straw nests, the foxes were tucking the cubs in, the badgers, noses towards the night sky, were sniffing the passing air outside the den for any impending danger ...the starlings began swirling around, patterning the sky like a giant's tattoo, moving shapes echoing the flights made by flocks of distant, distant relatives, alive long before they were even hatched!

The trees, branches facing East, the sign that it was time to rest.

All the birds and animals, even Herbert waited for the sun to pass down through the thickets and tall grass. As it did so it painted trails of orange and red light leaving the twilight colours to quiver on the surface of the river before disappearing into darkness. By which time, everyone on the riverbank, Herbert and Miss Lily included, were fast asleep...the only sound came from the chorus of industrious crickets who kept watch over crescent moon river. The speed of their clicks would indicate that someone or something unknown was approaching.

It was a mystery to Miss Lily and the townfolk, how the river never ran out of fish. Even though the fish returned to the river each and every day and Herbert got to fill his belly every single day and the townsfolk still made a living by selling the fish to other towns and villages far from the crescent moon river. The closest place was 'Djura'. 'Djuranians', murky creatures, lived there, obviously! More on them later. All we need to know now though is, that they really liked fish, trout to be more specific! And hunting...so a dinosaur and any fish gulping flying reptile was fair game to be hunted. This put Herbert in their sights. No wonder the old woman, her birds and that fish gorging flying dinosaur were the talk of the town.

The townsfolk also knew that before Herbert came along, there were very few fish in Crescent moon river , so , although they're were mutterings about the flying dinosaur and Miss Lily, they were quite satisfied with the regular fish haul from the river.

Herbert's eating habits and Miss Lily's limited space in her head of hair meant that eventually, the 'Herbert' situation would become untenable for all involved. The blue tits, geese, wrens, warblers and crows were quite looking forward to that! They instinctively knew, he was not one of them. Even though Herbert's diet was fish only, they all slept with one eye open Peering out from under their little wings just in case he developed a taste for something of the flying variety! Herbert's time with Ms Lily though, was nearing its end...

Miss Lily knew he would not be with her much longer. When Herbert was not flying or sleeping, he was clopping around on all fours, his claws thundering off the wooden floors like 100 horses galloping through the kitchen all at the same time his leathery wings knocked over teapots, plates, all the good China! He even bundled Miss Lily over a few times. No major damage done, thankfully!

She loved Herbert, clumsiness and all.

The whole time he felt very familiar to her.

She'd never had that feeling before with any of the birds that had nested in her hair.

Herbert, her husband, had been a paleontologist and lover of all things Cretaceous and Jurassic. He loved that Miss Lily loved birds. He would sit and watch her with her sketch book at the river's edge as the kingfisher plunged from its branch into the depths and returned with its silvery snack. She would sit, the nib of her pen scraping and scratching across the page until she was happy with her drawing.

Husband Herbert knew he was was not long for this world and would be dead soon, but he could not bring himself to tell Miss Lily. He was so torn it felt like he was splitting in two. So he made plans.. before it was too late.

The Creaking Parlour...A place for those who did not want to leave yet..

It was a wet, lonely Friday.

The cobbled pathway to the door was already flooded and ants and worms were struggling to get out of the path of the torrents coming towards them.

The sign above the door sneered down at Herbert, as it had done to all its clients, Herbert hunched his raincoat up and tried the door. It felt -as if something was pushing against him...something was pushing against him.

Herbert whispered, 'I need to come in, I don't have much time.'

The door released and Herbert stumbled in.

There was a counter, an old rusty cash register, an ink pad and behind the counter, a mountainous block of hundreds of little drawers with the name of every animal or creature you could think of, there was even a troll! Herbert had heard the rumours but now he was starting to believe.

A voice echoed through the front of the shop, 'You are here because? '

'My life is nearing its end,' said Herbert

'So you know what happens here then? said the voice

'I do.' Herbert shook, not from fear but reality had begun to set in.

'You must give me your body for the forest nutrients, and you must do a good deed for three , shall we say, people in the town, all of my choosing...

Well, two people, and one, em, ghost.

Person Number One was Mr. Wickenstaff the stealer of children's dreams.

He would steal the dreams of children when they were asleep.

Children who dreamt of becoming actors, doctors, film makers, writers, musicians, paleontologists, criminals, ahem, maybe not criminals, criminologists, scientists, speed skaters, waiters, bird keepers, deep sea divers, teachers... all stolen. Gone, never to be returned or fulfilled.

The town was full of unhappy, aimless, blank looking children slowly turning into hunched over adults with blackened eyes working mundane and horrible jobs such as packing hundreds of smelly or pongy fish for the next forty years over and over, every day for twenty hours, then sleep.

Then wake up, breakfast, fish packing then sleep. I'm

getting bored just writing this.

Mr Wickenstaff had his own dreams stolen at school when he was seven. He never recovered. I guess he was just passing it on.

Person Number Two was Mr Gravesby , the gravedigger. However, he was never actually seen burying bodies, digging holes yes, putting people in the holes after they had died, nope!

Mr Gravesby was in fact, the oldest and most sighted ghost in the town. Yet no one knew him. He was seen every single day, but every day, he was digging at a different spot.

The story goes that he had lost his wife in a tragic boating accident many many years before. Her body was never recovered or returned to him.

He died a broken soul. He now spends all of his time between worlds, searching for his wife, digging endless holes.

Person Number Three was Mrs.Trollfell who lived under the waterfall.

She eats....well....umm....gamers...yup, you heard it right... gamers.

The only reason I can come up with for this is that they are such easy targets. Think about it, they sit in their big fancy leather chairs all day, chewing on their fingers. They hide from the sunlight and turn their blood into liquorice by eating sugar all day!

Mrs. Trollfell was slow and a bit dim, but alas, she survived on the brains and livers of gamers...She used the eyes of the gamers as light bulbs... that glowed so brightly from watching the TV screens. Did you know that kind of light lasts after 50 years away from the body!

Lovely lady she was.

Once you have completed your deeds, said the voice, then and only then may you decide on your vessel.'

'How long do I get with her?' Herbert asked

'Thirty four days, only.' If you want to return again, I need another three good deeds for three more dreadful people. 'This shouldn't be a problem in this little town,' the voice sniggered and added 'know this! If you die during those thirty four days, you will be gone forevermore.'

Herbert nodded and repeated, 'Forevermore,' under his breath.

'When you die, please ensure you are in a state of rigor mortis so I can carry you easily,' the voice stated.

'I will,' Herbert said and then asked, 'do you know where I live?'

The voice let out a huge, hearty laugh, 'Mwoahahaha!'

Herbert backed slowly out the door and into the stormy, cold, wet evening.

He looked up, the drenched sign gave him a parting sneer... it was done,

Herbert pondered, Mr Wickenstaff. What do I need to do? I need to go back in time, he decided. I need to go back to his school days, the day his father told him he would amount to nothing.

Mr. Wickenstaff, or Seamus, as he was known to his friends, was very good at art. He would sit in the thickets and draw the scene as the day drew to a close. He was even able to draw the birds and other wildlife into his pictures even though they were constantly on the move. The woodmouse was his favourite. He loved its quirks and remarkable agility. He thought it industrious, 'Just like me,' he muttered to himself.

An art competition was on the Wednesday of that week. The competition was to 'Draw or paint a scene that you know the best'.

Seamus had been practicing every day for a month. He had decided he would paint his little spot down by the thickets where the woodmouse lived.

He spent hours drawing, longer than he had ever done paying careful attention to every little detail. Imagine, he spent three hours alone drawing one whisker on the side of the woodmouse's cheek!

Seamus' aunt, his father's sister, was particularly unwell during this time. Sadly, she passed away on the Sunday evening. Seamus had never seen his father so upset. His shoulders were hunched over. The bags under his eyes became puffed and black while his eyes were red from crying and lack of sleep. Seamus tried to think of ways to make his dad feel better. 'I know,' he said to himself ,'I'll show him my drawings for the Art Competition!' And so he did.

His father picked up the drawings in his huge, size of a spade, farmer's hands. He didn't have any more tears left although his eyes were still bloodshot from days of crying.

'Is this yours?' he quizzed Seamus.

'It's for a competition on Wednesday.'

'Have you been doing this instead of school work?'

'Well....'

Seamus didn't get a chance to answer before his father shoved the drawing into a drawer. He slammed it shut and bawled, 'Stop wasting your time on this rubbish Seamus, if you want to amount to anything! Now get out of my sight!'

His father slid back into his wooden chair; and back into his fog of his grief.

This stopped Seamus dead in his tracks.He knew his dad was so upset over his sister but....those words would live with him forever.

However, his broken story was about to change.

A little tornado had formed outside the Creaking Parlour. Yes, you guessed it, Herbert was now on his way to visit Seamus Wickenstaff.

Seamus was walking towards his father when from a gust of wind behind him a voice seemed to whisper, 'Wait a few days Seamus, just a few days.'

Seamus stalled. He slowly turned around and put his new drawings away in his drawer for a few days.

Seamus entered his drawings on Wednesday and soon after learned that he won. He told his dad expecting to be punished but instead he was delighted and they ate cake to celebrate!

Seamus would go on to become one of the most prolific artists of his time. Good Deed Number One done. Now for Good Deed Number Two, Mr Gravesby...the ghost in search of his wife.

'I need to find his wife. She is out at sea. She is out there somewhere,' he muttered out loud. Then he asked himself,' What are the most intelligent, biggest brained fish in the world?

'The Manta Ray! They are so calm, so intelligent and know every nook and cranny in every ocean in the world. *Manta* means blanket or cloak.'

What Herbert knew was that on request, manta rays could spread themselves like a blanket over the bottom of the ocean for miles and miles and miles like a huge duvet cover, embedded within it , are the most sensitive follicles, that could not only sense treasure like gold but also skeletons and the remains of the dead.

The most famous Manta Ray in the area was Bancroft... he'd been around since 1829. He was exactly 184 years old. Herbert met him on Thursday at the docks by the sail boats. His bushy eyebrows and lived in skin marked him out from the other young scullions in the area.

Herbert told him the story of Mr Gravesby.Bancroft listened and nodded, as if he knew the story already. Then, with one swift 'thwack' of his spiny tail, he was gone, gliding down into the pitch-black ocean.

Friday came. No sign of Bancroft. Saturday came. No sign of Bancroft.

Sunday morning came. Still no sign. At last Herbert saw bubbles breaking the surface. They got faster and bigger, and then Bancroft appeared like a huge submarine rising from the ocean floor, seawater gushing off the leathery skin on his back. Glinting in his mouth was a gold something. Upon inspection Herbert could see that it was a ring. And what's more it was engraved with this inscription, *'Eleanor Gravesby married Toby Gravesby,12/06/34'*

He had found her! Well, her ring anyway.

He thanked Bancroft with a bow and a tilt of his hat.

The next day, Herbert found Mr Gravesby, digging in his usual spot. Herbert, for the first time, noticed Mr Gravesby's transparency,and his aching sadness. He held out his hand, the ring in the centre of his palm.'I'm so sorry, ' he whispered.

Mr Gravesby bowed his head, picked up the ring. There was a howl of wind and he was gone.

Mr Gravesby was never again seen digging in the cemeteries of the town.

Now for the last, and final good deed, Herbert sighed. Mrs Trollfell. He decided to provide her with an endless supply of little gamers. She will never go hungry and it will never ever be dark in the town again... The local primary school, he knew, would have an endless supply of succulent little gamers for her!

One has to question whether this was actually a good deed? Right?

Herbert headed home

On seeing Miss Lily, Herbert's eyes welled up.

'I love you my dear.'

His voice disappearing into a whisper as he took very slow steps up to bed.

The next morning, Herbert was gone. His side of the bed was perfectly made. His books were stacked neatly and his coat lay over the arm of the chair.

All Miss Lily could do was sit by the edge of the Ginkgo forest and wait for him to return.

As she was waiting, she heard the cracking of what sounded like an egg. To her left she saw a little beak, well quite a long beak, poking out from this quite large, off colour, egg! Then, these tiny leathery wings appeared, and then, a fully formed baby Pterodactyl!

She recognised it straight away from Herbert's books.

'What the...!!!' she screamed. 'How is this even...' but before she could say anything more, the creature was curled up in a ball and sound asleep in her hand...

Herbert never returned.

Over the next few days, Miss Lily found at least five other baby chicks seemingly abandoned near the Ginkgo Forest. There was a barn owl chick and two baby swallows and a pair of blackbirds.

Over the next months , she found herself calling out for Herbert and the growing Pterodactyl would appear from nowhere!

Hmm, strange,she thought. And so it was...Herbert the Pterodactyl.

It was late evening on crescent moon river. The sun picked up the dust from the cut straw in the air. Everything shone gold or orange, even the river.

The fish were dead still in the water. They must have sensed Herbert's presence. Miss Lily sensed something else though, a movement in the tall grass beyond the riverbank..

Herbert swooped around from the otherside of the house and landed a few feet from Ms. Lily, perched on the riverbank, his claws buried deep into the river mud as he eyed up his late dinner under the surface. The fish remained motionless in the current.

Schooooooooooooooooop! Schooooooooooooooooop!

Miss Lily knew that sound all too well.. A Djuranian Arrow

- ones that could pierce rock. Anything in the way, had no chance. The first one missed Herbert by a hairs breath. The second one pierced his heart straight through.

'Nooooooooooooooooooooooooooooo!!!!' Ms Lily wailed, falling to her knees.

In slow motion, Herbert's wings folded. His body dropped into the water like a rock.The light in his eyes faded slowly.

Miss Lily darted to where he had fallen in. Her hand covered her mouth, her eyes filled with tears. Shaking, she couldn't take it in what had happened.

The silhouette of a man, a man she loved and adored, floated on down Crescent Moon river.

By Malcolm S Urquhart

2022

The End

Printed in Great Britain
by Amazon